President Amanda's Whistle-stop Trip

Dream!
Sue Pyatt

To Cindy, Daphne, Cobie, Tommy, Abigail, Taylor, Jade, Miss Dolly, BuddyCat, and rescue pets everywhere.

First Edition

ISBN 0-9742575-1-6

Printed in the United States of America

IMAGINATION STATION PRESS
–a subsidiary of Snowspring Ltd.
Arlington, Virginia

President Amanda's Whistle-stop Trip

By Sue Pyatt

Illustrated by Dana Saxerud

One morning in my White House bed,
I spring straight up to clear my head.

"It's time to hit the campaign trail."
Coolidge barks and wags his tail.

4

"We'll take a train from Imagination Station.
That's the way we'll tour the nation."

Before we leave, I call my dad and mother
--and, of course, my older brother.

I say, "I want to help **animals** as I travel on my train.
Animals will be the theme of my whistle-stop campaign."

"President Amanda," Freddie pleads, "I want to go."
I politely tell him, "No."

WHISTLE-STOP EXPRESS

WHISTLE-STOP DESTINATIONS
1. Baltimore, MD
2. Philadelphia, PA
3. New York City, NY
4. New Haven, CT
5. Cape Cod, MA
6. Chicago, IL
7. Yellowstone, WY
8. San Francisco, CA
9. San Diego, CA
10. Grand Canyon, AZ
11. New Orleans, LA
12. Everglades, FL
13. Charleston, SC
14. Home (The White House)
   Washington, DC

As my dream train departs a cloudy mist,
we announce the destinations on our list.

I'll speak for animals in every one.
Along the way we'll have some fun.

At the aquarium I have my wish
to stop a while and see the fish.

In my speech I'm quick to mention:
"Animals deserve attention."

n Franklin, one of our great sages,
as a founding father for the ages.

Independence Hall, I quote Ben and say,
Always ask, 'What good can I do today?' "

Be good to
animals here
on planet
Earth, and
recognize
each one has its
unique worth.

As we circle Manhattan in a boat,
the city's majesty I note.

To New Yorkers I shout, "Hooray!
My heart is with you all the way."

11

Whistle-stop 4:
New Haven, Connecticut

Yale students ask, as I expected,
"What will you do if re-elected?"

"I'll work hard for safety, seniors, and health care.
I'll work hard for schools, farmers, and clean air.

And yes, I'll work hard for every kid.
These are my promises for my re-election bid.

But on *this* trip as I see the country's sights,
I want to talk about animal rights."

Whistle-stop 5:
Cape Cod, Massachusetts

On Cape Cod I leave the campaign trail
and take time out to have a sail.

Whistle-stop 6:
Chicago, Illinois

We bike around Lake Michigan one sunny day.
Then we have our lunch at an avenue outdoor café.

Remember if you have a pet, it needs those checkups at the vet.

Whistle-stop 7:
Yellowstone National Park, Wyoming

Old Faithful shoots high above the park.
We stand and watch each blast 'til nearly da

The black bears, grizzlies, and the moose
have to lead a life that's loose.

Whistle-stop **8**:
San Francisco, California

We take the cable car to Pier 39
and find a seafood place to dine.

After that, we watch the fun
of sea lions basking in the sun.

15

A child inquires, "What will you do
to help the animals in the zoo?"

I say, "If as President I am again selected,
I'll work to keep our zoo animals protected."

Whistle-stop **10**:
Grand Canyon National Park, Arizor

At the Grand Canyon we hike and have a look.
From my pack I pull my bird and flower book.

Birds add to the Canyon's grandeur with their soaring grace.
Falcons, hummingbirds, and chickadees need a peaceful place.

The elk, deer, and bighorn sheep make this park their home.
They require vast open space where all can freely roam.

Whistle-stop 11:
New Orleans, Louisiana

At the parade, I climb aboard a float
and tell the crowd just how to vote.

21

The Everglades we need to treasure, or it won't remain a pleasure.

Fish, birds, and gators keep this park alive. We must restore their place to thrive.

23

Whistle-stop **13**:
Charleston, South Carolina

In a city with a timeless lure,
we slow down and take a carriage tour.

I am glad to see the care
our carriage driver gives his mare.

Here's what happens next:

I give my speech. Charleston cheers!
Coolidge spots a squirrel and disappears.

So, I have a problem in this dream,
but Mom and Dad are quickly on the scene.

Dad says, "Now, Amanda don't get shook.
I think I know just where to look."

At the shelter, I thank my lucky stars.
There is Coolidge, safe behind some bars.

"It's okay Cool," I say.
"I'll spring you right away."

As we walk by, many hopeful animals draw near
who are waiting for good families to appear.

At the Charleston shelter I am smitten
with a tiny, calico kitten.

We name him Charlie 'cause it's fittin'.

I claim Charlie as my own--
spring him, too, and take him home.

Whistle-stop 14:
The White House, Washington, D.C.

At my press conference, to Americans I suggest:
"Adopt from shelters. That's the best."

A few days later:

Dad runs in the Oval Office, newspaper in hand.
He booms, "The news today is surely grand!"

"Millions Adopt Shelter Pets," the headline blares.
"President Amanda, you have proved the country cares."

Here comes the magic end to my dream ride:
I win re-election in a landslide!

My family gathers around at my swearing-in.
Then I tell the country all the places I have been.

I speak to people all across our land,
about the second presidential term I've planned.

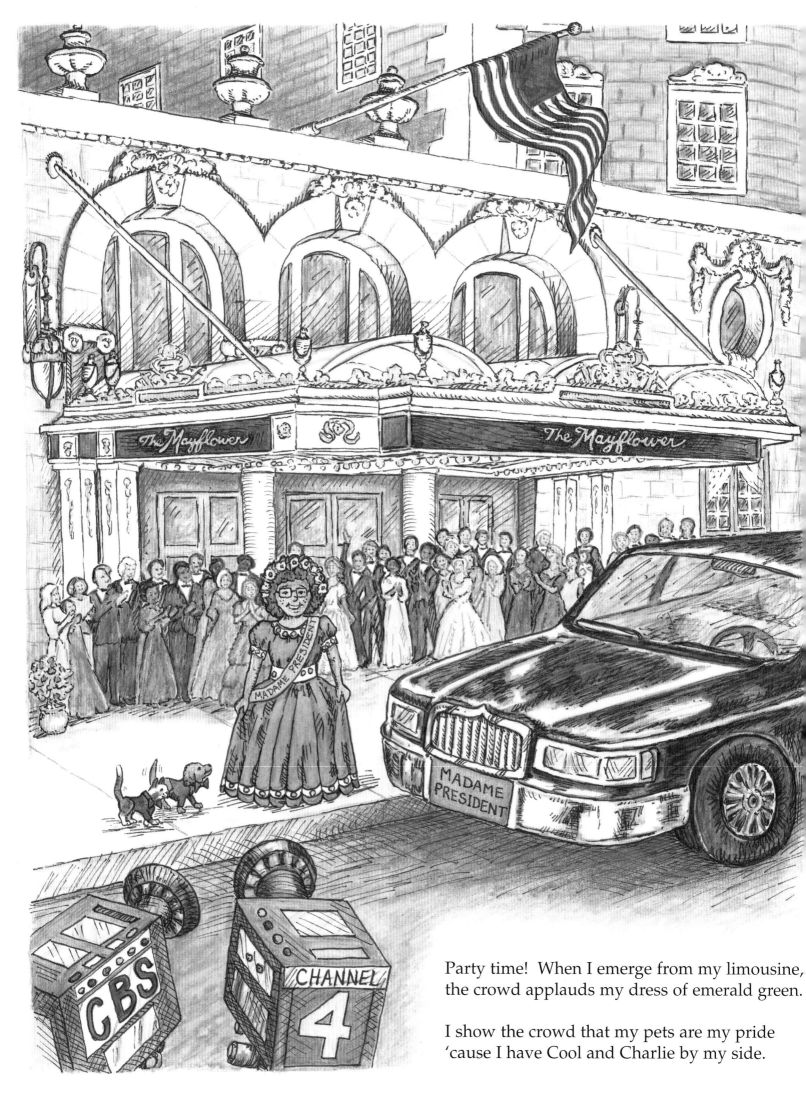

Party time! When I emerge from my limousine,
the crowd applauds my dress of emerald green.

I show the crowd that my pets are my pride
'cause I have Cool and Charlie by my side.

At my Inaugural bash in the Mayflower Hotel,
Dad says, "Amanda, you're the ballroom belle."

I say, "Dad, my dream wouldn't be just right,
without my family here to celebrate tonight."

THE END